Timothy, The Shooting Star

A Social Story About Autism

by

Christie Elam, EdD

Illustrations by Kalpart

Strategic Book Publishing and Rights Co.

Strategic Book Publishing and Rights Co., LLC
USA | Singapore
www.sbpra.com

For information about special discounts for bulk purchases,
please contact Strategic Book Publishing and Rights Co., LLC. Special Sales, at bookorder@sbpra.net.

ISBN: 978-1-948260-98-5

Timothy, The Shooting Star is the first book in the Savanna Tales series. The series focuses on the unique and sometimes challenging behaviors of children with emotional or behavioral disorders. The goal of this series is to help children connect to the characters in a way that embraces their differences and celebrates them as special and precious creations.

To my Lord and Savior who gives me strength to do all things.

A special dedication to Luke and all those who continue to overcome the challenges of autism. You are so special and have many wonderful things to share with the world.

To my Tony and sweet girls, Marissa and Braelynn.
I love you so much.

A special thank you to Mark Bernthal for your priceless wisdom and advice.

To my parents, family, and friends. Thank you for your continuous support.

Many thanks to Lynn, KJ, Bruce, Sherrill, and the staff at SBPRA Publishing for making this dream a reality.

Whoosh! Timothy the elephant enjoyed the soothing sound of the wind blowing through the tall grass as he walked to the river. He was alone yet again, but that was okay with him. He really didn't like spending time with the elephants or any of the other animals. As he continued his walk, he looked up at the sky and noticed the colors of the sunset starting to appear. He was thankful for this quiet moment alone.

He knew that very shortly he would arrive at the river where it wouldn't be so peaceful. All the other animals would be gathered there, and they made so much noise that it hurt Timothy's ears.

Loud noises and lots of movement gave Timothy a funny feeling inside. And that funny feeling made him do things. Weird things. Things like shaking his trunk back and forth wildly. He sometimes liked to make it look like a snake slithering in the grass. He didn't know why this made him feel better...it just did. But then the other animals would giggle and make fun of him. He felt sad when they did that.

12

Timothy knew he was different from the other animals. He didn't like to be the life of the party like Hannah the giraffe who was always telling funny jokes to the other animals. Timothy didn't even like to play games like Solomon the rhino, who loved to tackle and wrestle with his friends. Timothy just loved to be alone. Alone to think about his favorite subject—outer space. He knew everything about the solar system—the sun, the moon and all the stars. He could name every planet and constellation!

14

He saw the world differently. When the other animals looked at the moon, they just saw the moon. But when Timothy looked at the moon, he saw all kinds of round objects. Pictures would quickly flash through his mind. The eyes of a lion! The spots on a lizard! A drop of rain on a blade of grass! His mind worked like an amazing computer.

Timothy reached the river just after the sun went down. The noise from the other animals seemed louder than normal. It started as a slow drum beating in his ears and then the pounding went to his heart. Timothy started to feel weird. He didn't want to yell or do something silly, so he started thinking about outer space again to try to forget the feeling that was creeping into his trunk. It didn't work. The strange feeling became so strong that Timothy couldn't help it any longer. He started to wave his trunk in the air. The other animals looked at him.

Just as they started to laugh, a bright streak of light flashed across the sky. It was faster than Sampson the cheetah. The other animals were scared. Suddenly Timothy hollered, "It's okay, everyone! It's a shooting star!" The animals were shocked to hear him speak.

20

Everyone had so many questions for Timothy. Daniel the lion motioned for them to quiet down. The zebras knelt in the dirt, waiting to hear what Timothy had to say. The giraffes lowered their long necks to listen. Even the monkeys stopped their howling as they stared at Timothy.

"Can you tell us about the shooting star?" asked Daniel. Timothy looked down at his feet. It felt strange to look everyone in the eyes.

Timothy slowly started to talk as he continued looking at the ground. He began by explaining that what they'd just seen was the light from a dying star. Then he looked up and told them many things about the moon, the planets and the stars. He even pointed out the beautiful haze of stars called the Milky Way. The animals were surprised that Timothy knew so much. They thanked him for his lesson about the night sky.

Draw a picture of yourself. Be sure to include all the things that make you very special.

9 781948 260985